I got a message that I was to go and see the Qu...

"Herbert Fieldmouse," she said, "take this mes... to Baron VonGouda. It's...

TOP SECRET!"

DEDICATED

to my friends Cathy and Jamie,
their kids, Morgan and Jackson,
and . . . *Betty!*

TEXT AND ILLUSTRATIONS
copyright © 2003 by Kevin O'Malley
under exclusive license to MONDO Publishing

FOR INFORMATION CONTACT:
MONDO Publishing
980 Avenue of the Americas • New York, NY 10018
Visit our website at http://www.mondopub.com

Printed in China

03 04 05 06 07 08 09 HC 9 8 7 6 5 4 3 2 1
07 08 09 10 11 12 PB 9 8 7 6 5 4 3 2 1

ISBN 1-59336-042-8 (hardcover)   1-59336-043-6 (pbk.)

Designed by Cathy Evans

Library of Congress Cataloging-in-Publication Data

O'Malley, Kevin, 1959-
    Herbert Fieldmouse, secret agent / by Kevin O'Malley.
        p. cm.
    Summary: When Herbert Fieldmouse, secret agent, undertakes a secret mission for the
Queen, he finds that he must outwit the evil Dr. Whiskers.
    ISBN 1-59336-042-8 – ISBN 1-59336-043-6 (pbk. : alk. paper)
    [1. Spies--Fiction. 2. Undercover operations--Fiction. 3. Mice--Fiction. 4. Cats--Fiction.
5. Humorous stories.] I. Title.

PZ7.O526He 2003
[E]--dc21
2003046430

So there I was on another secret mission.
It was cold. It was dark. I knew I was
being followed by…

THE EVIL DR. WHISKERS!

30TH STREET
TRAIN STATION

SERVICE
ENTRANCE

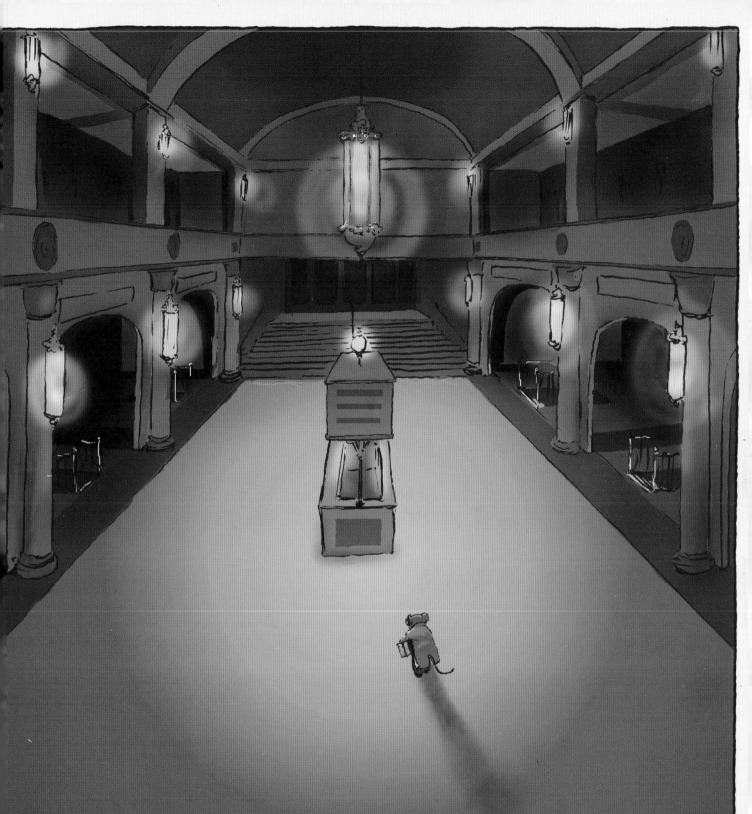

The train station was quiet—too quiet. I made my way to the train, and for some reason I had that feeling you get when you don't study for a test ... but you tell your mom that you did.

Maybe it was my
frame of mind. Maybe it
was the cheese. But something smelled
rotten. Wait a minute ... I knew that smell—

SOUR MILK!

I turned. I was too late. We passed through a tunnel and Dr. Whiskers got the jump on me!

We struggled...
   but I had let my guard down.
   Dr. Whiskers grabbed the box.

I took up the chase, following him to the top of the racing locomotive–but I was too late. The foul-smelling Dr. Whiskers ESCAPED!

And with him went the Queen's SECRET MESSAGE

Maybe I should have been a church mouse. But hey, I'm a secret agent. It's a job and it pays the rent.

Anyhow, I had to get that letter back. So I headed down the other side of the tracks to a scratching post called

LITTLE PERSIATOWN.

I went to see Big Tabby, the fat cat who runs Little Persiatown.

"Where's Dr. Whiskers?" I asked.

"Why should I tell you, Fieldmouse?" questioned Big Tabby.

"'Cause if you don't, I'll close down this illegal catnip operation of yours so fast it'll make your tail spin."

That got Big Tabby's tongue moving.

He told me so much about Dr. Whiskers's

place that it felt like I was talking to some

sort of evil travel agent. Anyhow, I headed

down to the pier. I was looking for a Siamese

cat named Pasha and her boat the

Quivering Whisker.

The place wasn't
hard to find.

PASHA'S BOAT RENTAL

PASHA'S
BOAT
Rental

Sail THE
Quivering
Whisker

Day, Weekend,
or Evening

$3 per
hour

Hours of
Operation
8:36
to
12:23
Thursday
through
Sunday

TRIPS
TO THE

$50

EVIL
ISLAND

NIGHTS
ONLY

OF

DR. WHISKERS

13

I went into Pasha's shop. I nosed about for a while and then rang the bell for assistance. A voice behind me said, *"May I help you?"* I spun around . . .

and there stood the most beautiful cat I had ever seen!

She must have thought I was okay too, 'cause she agreed to go to dinner with me that night. After the important stuff was out of the way, we talked about business.

"I need your boat to get to

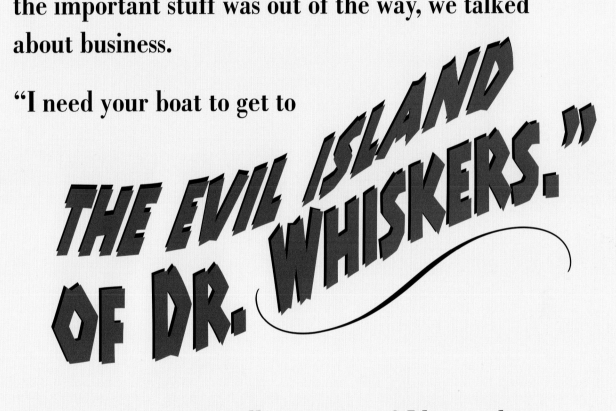
THE EVIL ISLAND OF DR. WHISKERS."

"Are you sure you really want to go? I have taken many to that island, but I have never brought anyone back," Pasha purred.

"Thanks for the warning, but I've got a job to do."

Later that night we headed for **THE EVIL ISLAND OF DR. WHISKERS.** The sight of the castle gave me the

CREEPS!

Maybe I should have listened to Pasha after all. But I had to get that secret message back—it's my job.

"Don't go," whispered Pasha.

"Wait for me," I said.

"You won't come back," she cried.

"Wait for me," I said.

I started to climb.
I looked back
down and...

PASHA WAS GONE!

Once inside,

I crept down a
long hallway.
I got the feeling,
you know, like
I was being
watched.

I went through a second door—

MOUSETRAPS!!

And in the center of the room was the SECRET MESSAGE.

I had worked my way across the room when **SUDDENLY THE LIGHTS WENT OUT.** *I could smell ... SOUR MILK.*

"**OPEN THE BOX**," hissed Dr. Whiskers.

He could see me but I couldn't see him...
he had **CATVISION!**

"Anything you say," I replied.

This time I was ready for his trickery—I had loaded the box with tennis balls. I opened it, grabbed the Queen's letter, and then threw the balls into the air. Mousetraps snapped like peanut brittle.

I headed out the way I came in. I emptied a
bag of *kitty litter* by the door. Cats love
the stuff. They can't stop themselves from
pawing at it.

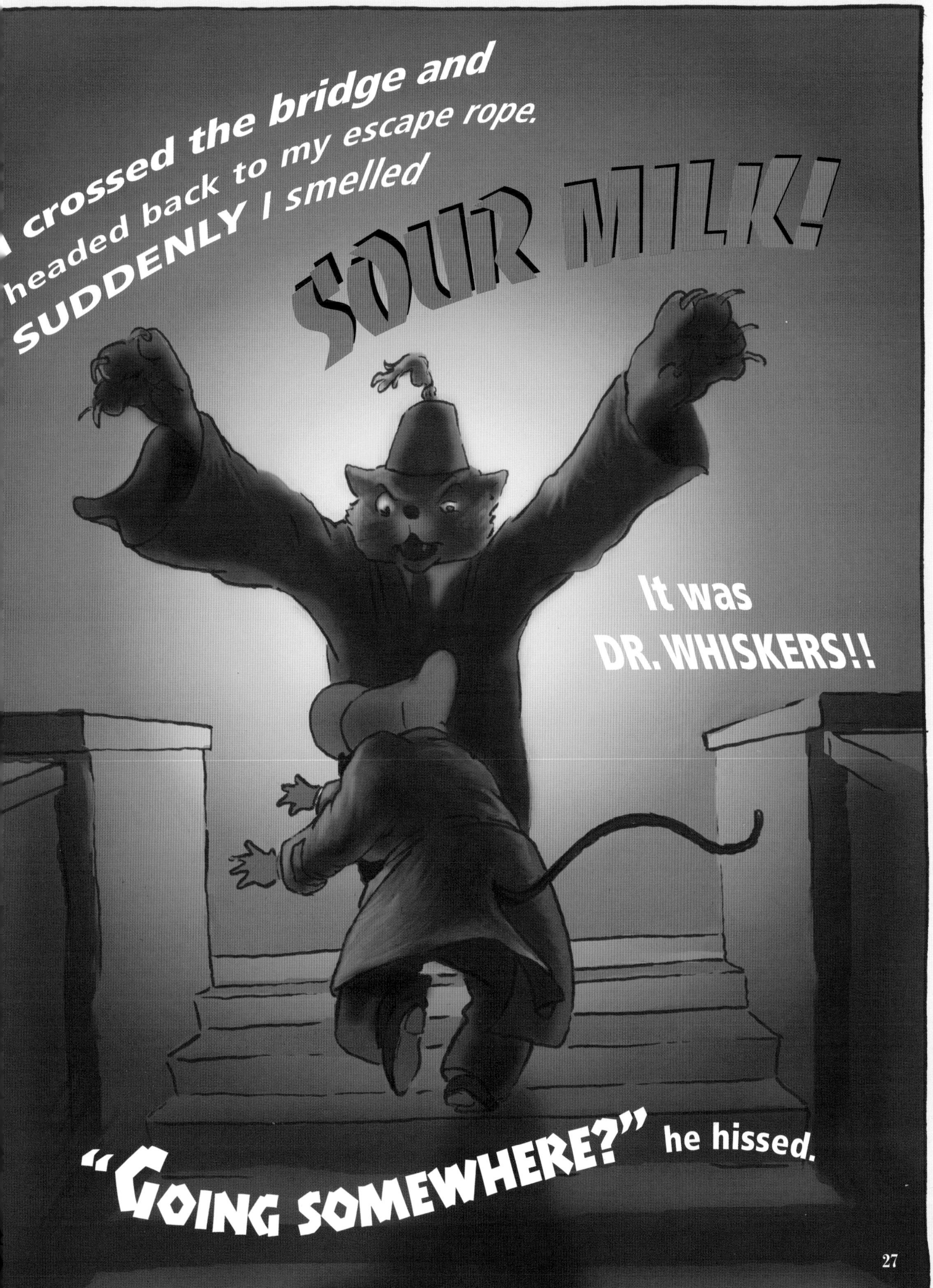
I crossed the bridge and
headed back to my escape rope.
SUDDENLY I smelled
SOUR MILK!
It was
DR. WHISKERS!!
"GOING SOMEWHERE?" he hissed.

I used my last secret weapon—

a toy mouse filled with

catnip. I dangled it in front of his
eyes and then tossed it off of
the bridge. Without a thought, he took the bait and
went over the side of the bridge. I raced back to my
rope and climbed down.

You know cats, though. They've got nine lives.

SMELLED DR. WHISKERS AGAIN!!

Too bad about Pasha. It looked like

I WAS TRAPPED!

SUDDENLY there was the ROAR of an ENGINE!

It was **PASHA!**
I jumped for the boat just as Dr. Whiskers jumped for me.
Splash! Wet cat!

"Thanks, Pasha," I said.

I was falling in love with that kitten. Who would have guessed…a cat and a mouse. Anyhow, Pasha dropped me off at Baron VonGouda's place and I delivered the secret message.

Dear Baron,
You left your umbrella here after lunch. Shall I return it?

Regards, The Queen

Some big **secret message**, huh? I'll tell you, about now, being a church mouse sounds pretty good.